IN MY HEAD

ALICIA RADES

1

I regain consciousness just in time to panic. I can't see anything, and suddenly every nerve in my body goes into overdrive. My body shakes as I reach out for my father.

"Dad!" I cry. I know he's there somewhere. My arms flail as I try to find something to ground me to reality.

A moment later, I feel hands clamp around my wrists. "It's okay," I hear my father's voice say.

"Dad!" I whisper breathlessly. I blink a few times until the room comes back into focus. The glowing computers outline my father's silhouette.

"Mila," my father says as he pulls me close to his belly. He seems so tall because he's standing and I'm still half sitting, half lying on the table. "Mila, you're fine. What's all the fuss about? You've done this a million times."

He's right. I *should* be fine. This is the twelfth upgrade I've had in the past ten years. Never before had I woken with such an odd sensation. What if this time is different?

I calm my breathing as I press my head against my father's body for comfort. I bite back tears that threaten in response to the terror I just felt but can't explain. I don't cry. Dad runs his hands through my dark hair as he assures me I'm going to be okay.

"Her heart rate spiked there for a little bit, but she looks fine now," J.P. says from across the room. He's Dad's intern. Well, kind of. J.P. goes to school with me but is two years older. He's enrolled in an apprenticeship program where he learns about Mahone Inc.'s system while he's still in school. It's supposed to cut down on his time in college.

Of course, the heart rate monitor is only a precaution. No one ever really needs it. Since I was six, I never needed it. Until now.

"Are you okay, Mila?" Dad asks as he pulls away from me and looks over my face to assess my reaction.

I press a hand to my head. "Yeah," I answer. "I feel fine. I don't know what all that was about. I'm sorry."

"Don't be sorry, Mila," my father insists. "If something is wrong with this version of the program, we have to know before we release it to the public."

Part of me feels proud that Dad is the chief technology manager at Mahone Inc. It means that I get to beta test the latest upgrades to the chip in my head. This time, it's a full-fledged hardware replace instead of just a software update. It's not like they have to cut into me, though. The chip is actually partially outside the body. I'm not entirely sure how it works, but I know that if you look at the base of someone's neck, you can see their implant.

Of course, everyone I know has one, but Dad says there are still people outside the city who just don't have the money or don't want one, although I can't see why anyone wouldn't want one. I guess they're afraid of a government conspiracy or something, like the implant can read your thoughts, but it doesn't read *all* your thoughts, just the commands you give your devices. And besides, Dad says there's no way to store the commands we give, so it's not like anyone can be monitoring our brains and using it against us.

Plus, the implants have such a short range. Like, if I want to tell the thermostat at home to turn up the heat, I have to communicate with my watch first to get the signal to reach that far. Still, I'm really looking forward to everything I'll be able to do with this upgrade.

At the same time, I resent it. In the beginning, it only alienated me from my classmates. Since my dad works with Mahone and we have the money, I was the first of my classmates to get the implant, the one that would connect me to The Internet of Things. My classmates were all jealous of how I could communicate with my home and my devices without lifting a finger, so they decided to shut me out. J.P. is the only person I can be seen with because we're in the same boat. His dad works for Mahone, too. But I wouldn't exactly call J.P. and I friends. Besides our dads' professions, we have nothing in common.

But, of course, I can't tell my dad any of this. Letting him know how much I hate his job because it means I don't have any friends would only break his heart. And I know getting the latest upgrade isn't going to make people hate me any more than they already do. So I don't let it show. And besides, I *do* feel fine. It must have just been nerves because of the full hardware upgrade.

I force a smile. "Really, Dad. I am fine. I can't wait to get home and see how this version feels."

Dad smiles back, and I can see J.P. out of the corner of my eye forcing a smile of his own. J.P. seems unsure about my words, but my dad looks like he believes me, and that's all that matters right now.

"Okay." Dad gives me a quick kiss on the forehead. "I'll see you at home. I love you, Mila."

"Love you, too, Dad."

I jump down from the table, grab my bag, and sling it

over my shoulder. "Bye." I wave to the other people in the room before I leave.

I ride the elevator down to the first floor and walk across the street near the Fountain. The Fountain is this big courtyard area in the middle of the city where tons of people hang out. There are mostly big corporation buildings surrounding it, but there are cafés and shops in their lower levels, so groups of people are always sitting along the edge of the trickling fountain.

I spot a few people from school hanging out nearby. Blonde hair and an attractive smile from the cutest guy in the group sends my heart fluttering. That's Carter. I don't think he sees me, but I lean down to unlock my bike and let my hair conceal my face anyway so that I don't have to meet my classmates' eyes.

I could use my car if I wanted to—the one Dad bought me a few years ago—but I prefer my bike. It's the best way for me to get my exercise in. Dad used to tell me that years ago, people would have to operate their cars manually kind of like how I operate my bike, but now they're self-driving. Dad even told me that people once needed to go through classes and get licenses to drive cars. That seems kind of silly to me.

Dad tells me a lot of stories about the olden days, how things were when he was young. When I was little, he used to tell me about the crazy amount of energy people would use and that it was actually warming up the world. Global warming, they called it. Crazy, isn't it?

But it's not like that anymore. I guess somewhere along the way, people realized things needed to change. And it's ironic. Even though our implants have helped get rid of the mundane things about life, people have become more active and involved in things. Like, we have full capabilities to have everyone go to school online, but no one wants to be completely secluded or study alone, so we don't really do that anymore. And even though we have cars to take us places, most people like me ride on their bikes when it's not too far because it saves us energy.

Dad's stories have always fascinated me.

I pedal at a moderate pace back home. It isn't too far —just a few miles. Despite my anxiety from earlier, I'm anxious to use the new tech Dad is beta testing on me, so on the way home, I try out a few tricks on my watch. Without saying a word, I bring up the GPS app and have it guide me home. I notice almost immediately how much smoother communication seems and how quick the response time is.

Of course, I don't need the GPS app because I know my way home. I look out across the landscape. The tall buildings of the city are already behind me, and I can see the wind turbines rotating in the distance. Glimmers of light shine off the solar panels of the one- and two-story houses.

I decide to test out a different app on my watch, telling it to launch my music. Suddenly, something hard hits my head, so hard that I fall off my bike and it skids across the sidewalk. I throw my hands beneath me, but they do little to catch my fall. I skin my elbow. It stings, but it's nothing that can't be fixed easily.

The pounding in my head doesn't stop. I squeeze my eyes shut tight to ease the thumping, but that doesn't seem to work.

Quiet, I think.

Just like that, the pounding in my head transforms into a low melodic tune.

Oh. After a second, I realize what's happening.

Of course. My father briefed me about this aspect before I went in for the upgrade. Why didn't I listen closer? He had said that instead of audio playing through my watch speakers, it would come through the implant and play as if it was in my head. Genius, really, but I could have used a little more of a forewarning, like, *Mila, if it feels like your head is being cracked open, don't worry. That's just music.*

I roll my eyes at the thought then laugh a little at myself for being so afraid of the music. I climb back on my bike and let the music get louder in my head. As I pedal back home, I decide the music is really pretty cool.

It's definitely something I'm going to take notes on for the beta test.

I just hope that heart-rate spike hadn't meant anything. I didn't want to ruin Dad's data.

But I feared I already had.

2

As I near home, I start testing my new tech right away. Dad said this one would have a farther range, so I give a few commands as I approach the front gate around our property. The gate springs open much sooner than I anticipated, and I smile at how cool that is. I test the same thing on our front door and get the same result.

"How'd it go?" my mom asks when I walk in the door. She's already waiting for me in the foyer, and she's holding out a tray of cookies.

"It went fine," I tell her as I grab a cookie from her tray. They're warm and delicious.

I try to imagine my mom with flour on her face and dough on her hands the way people used to cook in the olden days. Dad tells me about that all the time. But I've never even seen flour, so I don't really know how to picture it. Dad says people used to *bake from scratch.* Now all the food delivered to our door is prepackaged. We could order cookies that are already cooked, but Mom likes to bake, so she only orders the frozen dough. I think Mom would be a great cook given the right ingredients, but I honestly can't even see her spreading peanut butter on a piece of bread. That's what they used to do back in the olden days. It sounds like a tasty treat to me.

"That's good to hear," my mom says.

We head toward the kitchen together, me in the lead. She walks slower than I do—she always has ever since she broke her leg when I was little. I still remember the day vividly. It was the day after I got my first implant, and she was playing with me in the living room when the phone rang. She went upstairs to talk in private and came running back a few minutes later, only to trip on the top step and break her leg on the way down.

My mother's voice pulls me from the memory. "I mean, I didn't expect anything to go wrong. It never does. But I just want to make sure it went all right."

My mom already received her beta upgrade. I wonder briefly if she experienced something odd, too, but I know she would have said something if she did.

"Yeah, Mom. Things went fine like always."

"Mila!" my mom exclaims in alarm.

I whirl around to face her. "What?"

"What happened to your arms?" She points to my elbows.

"Oh," I say, cradling the scrape on my right elbow. "I fell off my bike. The music app scared me."

My mom laughs out loud. "It scared me the first time, too."

It's Saturday, so I don't have school. I quickly scan the screen on the door of the refrigerator with my eyes to see what we have. There's one column that shows what we have in the fridge and another that lists what we're out of and is coming in our grocery shipment on Sunday.

Dad used to tell me about how people actually had to go to the grocery store and shop for themselves. Can you believe it? Now our refrigerator analyzes what we have and creates an automatic order that's shipped to our front door each week. Of course, the refrigerator only orders our regular items, but we can add extra things to the order ourselves, like if we were hosting a party—if we ever actually had parties.

I quickly try the refrigerator function out. We don't normally have orange juice, so I mentally tell the fridge to add it to the list. It does. Then I reach into the fridge and grab one of my lunches. I stick it in the oven and mentally set the temperature and time.

I turn and see Mom looking at me. Her tray of cookies sits on the counter, and she's chewing on one. "J.P. was there, I trust?" Mom says after she swallows.

"Well, yeah," I say like she's just asked the dumbest question in the world. I know she's teasing me.

Mom raises her eyebrows.

"Mom," I scold. "Would you stop it? J.P. and I are barely even friends. We're both losers, and we know it, but that doesn't mean we get along."

Mom has been rooting for us to get together for ages, but no matter how many times I explain it to her, she still doesn't understand that even though J.P. and I sit together at lunch, we aren't exactly friends.

I'd love to have friends, to be part of the popular crowd, but I don't. Sometimes I feel like I'd do practically anything to fit in. Anything, that is, but risk disappointing my father. Not to add that I know it'd be impossible to get into Ariel's crowd.

"Oh, honey. You're not a loser," my mom assures me.

Luckily, the stove dings just then to tell me my lunch is ready, so I don't have to explain to my mother just how much of a loser I am. I shove my food in my mouth so I don't have to talk.

"Slow down, Mila. That's not healthy."

I roll my eyes at her, and she takes it as a cue to stop pestering me. Instead, she announces she's going for a dip in our pool.

After I'm done eating, I toss my dish in the recycling and head to my room to test out my new tech. I try the shower first and notice it's quick to respond to my commands for a temperature change. Dad already installed new chips in all the appliances in the house as part of the beta test, so all of us and our house are compatible now.

My watch is still attached to my wrist, and I tell it to play music again so I can get used to the new feature. I jump a little when it starts playing in my head, but this time, I'm prepared. I listen to the music as I shower, and it plays my favorite song. I close my eyes and sing along.

Then, just for a brief moment, I feel a cool breeze pass over my skin. Shivers travel down my spine, even though I'm under the warm water.

I tell the music to stop, and I poke my head out of the shower to see if my mom opened the door, but I'm alone.

Weird, I think. *I must be imagining things.*

Still... I can't shake the chill tingling down my spine telling me it's something else entirely.

3

J.P. and I sit in silence at the lunch table. It's like this every day. He sometimes opens his mouth like he wants to say something, but he never does. Today, he keeps his eyes down and on his food.

I let my eyes wander across the lunchroom. I notice some kids glaring and pointing at me from a few tables away. The guy who picks his nose and sits alone at the table next to mine is staring at me funny. Even the genius kid who sits behind me in math has his eyes locked on me.

It must be because of my new implant. It glows a slightly brighter blue on the back of my neck than everyone else's does. I casually reach up and pull out my ponytail elastic so my dark hair will conceal the implant. I'm not sure how casually I manage it as my eyes dart around the room uncomfortably. I'd rather look anywhere but at the group of kids staring at me.

"Don't worry about them," J.P. says. "They're just jealous. They want the upgrade, too."

I nod like I understand, but I really don't know why they need to point and stare.

"What about your upgrade?" I ask.

"I don't have it yet. Remember?"

Right. J.P. was part of this round's control group. Working at Mahone didn't always have its privileges. They needed some people to look at the data objectively without testing it on themselves and getting biased feedback. J.P. used to get the upgrades the same time I did, but not since he started apprenticing with them at the beginning of the year.

We sit in silence for another few minutes. It's only ever small talk with us, if that. In the silence, I think about what happened to me yesterday and briefly wonder what it means. Perhaps J.P. could look into it for me. After lunch, he's headed straight for the Mahone offices. It's part of the apprenticeship program where he gets to skip out on the last half of school and still get credit for working there.

"You have access to my data, right?" I ask J.P. boldly. Normally I wouldn't discuss private things like this with him, but the only alternative is to ask my dad, and I don't want to worry him.

"Yeah, I do." He nods as he touches the back of his neck. His fingers lightly brush the end of his dark brown hair, and his shirt tightens across his surprisingly muscular chest. For a long time, I thought he did this just to make sure his implant was still there or something, but I've learned it's just a habit of his.

"Can you check mine today?" I ask.

He shakes his head. "I shouldn't be accessing your data."

"Please," I beg. "I just want to make sure everything's all right."

Alarm enters his tone. "Is something wrong with your implant?"

I think about the way it made me feel when I woke up after surgery. I can't place my finger on it, but something just didn't feel right.

"I'm not sure," I admit. "I just want to make sure everything is okay after that weird heart rate spike yesterday. Will you help me?"

He hesitates a moment, before saying, "I'll help the best I can."

Cheers erupt from the other end of the cafeteria. We both look to see Carter Hayes high-fiving his group of friends. Carter is arguably the hottest, most popular guy in my grade, so when I say that he high-fived his friends, I basically mean his entire corner of the lunchroom. People gather around him, but I can't see what's going on. Even some of the popular guys from the older grades crowd around his table.

I can't help but lock my eyes onto Carter. If I weren't such a reject in this school, I might be able to talk to him. Just looking at him makes my insides go soft and my heart flutter.

Ariel Wright clings to his arm and smiles up at him like he's a god. I grit my teeth in annoyance. She's surrounded by tons of people, including Trish Spencer, who has been her best friend since the first grade… ever since Ariel ditched me.

Arial and I were friends once. Then I got my first implant, and she turned everyone against me. That was back when we were six, but still, I can't help but hate her, seeing how my social status clearly never recovered.

I don't know what all the cheering is about until Carter turns and I notice the light blue glow on the back of his neck. It's lighter than everyone else's, except mine.

"How did he get an upgrade?" I mumble, not really expecting an answer.

"Randomly chosen," J.P. says. "He was one of our randomly selected beta testers."

"I don't get it," I say, narrowing my eyes. "I have the upgrade, too, and people just stare and whisper. Why are they cheering for him?"

J.P. just shakes his head, like he can't quite make sense of it, either.

Just then, my watch buzzes, and the entire lunchroom goes silent. Everyone is glued to their devices, and I know instantly that this is a mass message.

Dad told me about a new feature with my upgrade, so I try it out. I mentally tell my watch to read me the message, and a computer-generated voice enters my head.

"Who doesn't love fun in the sun?" it says excitedly. *"No one, that's who!"*

"It's playing *in my head!*" Carter exclaims across the lunchroom, and people start cheering for him again.

The computer voice continues relaying the announcement. *"Join us for a pool party this Saturday, three p.m. at 1113 Mulberry Lane. Anyone and everyone is welcome."*

1113 Mulberry Lane. I know that address. That's Ariel Wright's house. I bite down on my lip and try to make sense of this announcement.

"You look confused," J.P. says.

"I know Ariel throws parties often, but she's never invited everyone," I explain. "Is this some new way to try to boost her popularity even more?"

J.P. looks at me like it's obvious. "Homecoming."

Oh. Ariel is trying to win brownie points so everyone will vote her the sophomore class's homecoming representative. Well, I won't, I tell you. I won't attend her stupid *I'm queen of the world* party, either.

But, then again, she did say everyone is invited. Lots of people will be there, and if I'm there with them, it might actually win *me* some brownie points in the social hierarchy here at school. Maybe showing I'm not all that bad or different could make people like me more despite getting upgrades before them.

"Don't even *think* about it," J.P. says. His brown eyes stare into mine seriously.

The thoughts in my mind must be showing on my face. "Think about what?" I ask innocently, even though I know exactly what he's talking about.

"It's not going to make them like you any more," he tells me.

"Well, it can't make them like me any less," I argue.

"I'm telling you that you shouldn't go."

Heat rises to my face, and suddenly, I want to go now more than ever. "Who are you to tell me what to do?"

"Ariel is practically your arch enemy," J.P. points out.

I narrow my eyes at him. "What would you know about that?"

He holds his hands up defensively. "Hey, I'm just trying to be a good friend."

"Friend? I don't have any friends. That's why I should go to this pool party." I try to keep my voice down, but I'm sure half the lunchroom hears me. I stand from my seat angrily and head across the lunchroom to recycle my dishes. Where does J.P. think he has any right to tell me what to do?

When I turn after dumping my tray in the trash, my eyes lock briefly on Carter's. He stares back with a half-smile. My cheeks flame, and I turn away, letting my loose hair conceal my face. I escape from the lunchroom as quick as I can.

At least if I go to this pool party, one good thing might come from it.

I might actually work up the courage to talk to Carter.

4

J.P. and I don't talk much at lunch the rest of the week, not that we normally do. He tells me my readings look normal, but that he'll give it a closer look. Then he tries talking me out of the party again. I can't help but snap a snarky comment back at him. Why doesn't he want me to go?

After that, his silence only makes me angrier at the notion that he thinks he can boss me around.

At lunch that week, I'm reminded of the announcement that came on Monday, and I spend my time daydreaming about how the pool party will go. I don't know what to wear, so on Wednesday, I do some shopping on my watch—which turns out to be really cool with the new implant—and order a new bikini. It comes in the mail on Thursday, and when I try it on, it looks great. It has a single strap across the right shoulder and is made of a silver metallic fabric. There's even a cute white dress coverall that came with it.

I tell Mom about the pool party, and she seems more than happy about it. At sixteen, I'm finally attending my first party! Her excitement only fuels my own.

Later, Mom and I test out the calling function on our new implants. She stands at one end of the house, and I stand at the other. It's incredible how we can hear each other's voices in our own minds, but we still have to speak out loud to make it work.

On Friday night, Dad sends me a link to a new article about the olden days. It's too intriguing to pass up, so I tell my implant to read aloud to me. I listen to the article about the history of the telephone while I float carelessly on a tube in our pool.

The article finishes, and I wonder if I should bring this tube to the pool party, or order another one. Maybe it's best if I don't bring one at all. I pull up a shopping app on my phone and start to browse pool tubes.

A voice cuts through the silence. I check my watch to see what's playing, but nothing appears on the screen. I listen closer.

"Don't go to the pool party."

I'm caught so off-guard that I wobble a little on the inner tube, then topple over into the pool. I'm not in the deepest part, but I still gasp for air as I come back up.

"What!?" I practically scream. I look around my yard nervously, but there's no one around.

I focus on the voice's words, which sound a lot like J.P.'s, only it clearly wasn't J.P.'s voice in my head. It was a guy, I could tell, but that was all I could make out. I thought about who even knew I was going to the pool party, and I realized anyone in the lunchroom could've overheard mine and J.P.'s conversation.

"Who's there?" I say out loud, only no one answers.

The weird thing is that if someone was in my head, the only explanation I had was that they were communicating by calling me, but I would have to answer the call first. Plus, when Mom and I tested it, there was this background static that would tell you that you were on a call. I didn't feel that this time.

I dry myself off and head toward my room. I must've imagined it. It had to be my subconscious agreeing with J.P., but I don't care. I'm still going to the party.

I consider telling Dad about it, but if it really was my imagination, then that would screw up his data. I decide to keep this one to myself just for now.

On Saturday, three o'clock can't come soon enough. I spend the day trying out different hairstyles, which unfortunately gives me too much time to think about my decision. Part of me wants to agree with J.P. and skip the party altogether, but then I think about how this could be my chance to make real friends.

I decide I won't chicken out, but I still don't know how to do my hair. Should I put it up or leave it down? I don't want to make it seem like I'm showing off my upgrade, but then again, everyone cheered when Carter showed off his. Maybe everyone at the party will think my upgrade is just as cool. I can't be sure.

I decide to put my hair up but in a way that's easy to let down if I start getting odd stares. I tell my watch to display easy updos, and it shows an enlarged holographic screen in front of my face. I flip through different styles before I settle on one.

"I'd keep your hair down," a voice says in my mind.

At first, I think it's an ad playing off the website I'm on; I've gotten used to that the past few days. Then I realize that it's the same voice I heard in the pool.

"Who are you?" I demand out loud. The voice doesn't sound familiar, so I'm sure it's not someone I know. It's clearly a male voice, though.

"Just a friend."

"A friend? If you were a friend, you'd stay out of my head. I should be able to tell if I'm on a call with you, and I'm not. Who are you?"

"You can call me Parker."

I must be imagining the voice. It doesn't sound

computer generated, and I don't hear the quiet static in the background that would tell me I'm on a call. Perhaps my intense feeling for needing friends has made me go crazy, and that terrifies me. Only more reason to go to the party and make some friends.

"I don't need a friend," I tell Parker, but I know it's a complete lie. "Stay out of my head."

Parker doesn't say another word, so I figure he's gone. I'm about to put my hair up when I decide to leave it down. I want to appear approachable.

I just hope going to this party isn't a big mistake.

5

I don't leave until three o'clock so that I'm not the first one there. I consider taking my car, but I don't want it to seem like I'm trying to show off even more than people think I already do, so I decide to take my bike. Mom gives me a hug goodbye and tells me to enjoy myself.

When I ride up to 1113 Mulberry Lane, the driveway is already packed with cars and bicycles. Someone says hello to me as I enter the house, but it's so crowded that I can't tell who greeted me. I plaster a smile on my face to make it look like I'm enjoying myself, but all my insides have turned to fire as I nervously wonder how to fit in. A lot of people have drinks in their hands, so I make my way to the kitchen to grab a glass.

Out the window, I can see another crowd of people

around the pool. Some are swimming, and there are girls tanning on the patio. Ariel's house is smaller than mine, but her pool must be twice the size. All I can hope is that she doesn't spot me at her party, because I know she wouldn't want me here. With so many people around, I doubt she'll see me, though.

I pour myself a glass of fruit punch and continue scanning the backyard through the window. I spot a game of volleyball going on out in the lawn. I've never been one for sports, but there are a group of girls I recognize from school watching the game. I figure I can try talking to them. They look like the type of girls I could get along with.

I push through the crowd and out toward the volleyball court. The five girls I spotted from the kitchen haven't moved. When I approach them, one of the girls turns. She has short bright red hair and fair skin.

"Um, do you mind if I sit here?" I ask, gesturing to a spot on the grass. I know I don't really have to ask, but I don't want to intrude on their group, either.

The girl with the red hair smiles as the other four girls shift their gazes toward me. "That's fine with us. You're Mila, right?"

I nod as I sink to the ground.

"I'm Kaya," she says with a big smile. "This is Em, Anya, Callie, and Patrice."

"Hi," I greet everyone. They seem nice enough as

they all smile back. I inch a little closer to their group, and they don't seem to mind.

"We were just guy watching," Kaya explains. "Who do you think is the hottest one?" She gestures toward the court.

"Um..." I say as I eye the boys on either side of the net. They're all pretty muscular, and they *all* have their shirts off.

One guy with blonde hair dives into the grass to bump up the ball, and my eyes lock on him. *Carter.* Heat rises to my cheeks. It's not like he would go for me or anything, but my goodness, he is gorgeous.

"Oh, I see," Kaya says teasingly. "Say no more." Then she turns toward her other friends. "Mila votes for Carter, so that puts him in the lead."

"What?" I practically squeak. "I never even answered."

Kaya shrugs. "You didn't have to."

They all laugh, and for a moment, it feels like they're laughing *at* me. I sit with them a while longer, but all they do is talk about guys I don't know, and I feel a little left out. When the guys on the court decide to take a break, I also stand up and leave. The girls next to me hardly even notice.

I spot Ariel by the pool as I head back inside. She hasn't seemed to notice yet that I'm here, and I'm grateful for that. We haven't spoken in years, but I don't know what she'd think if she knew a loser was attending her pool party. I'm comforted by the thought that she's working on schmoozing all her pool mates to win the spot on homecoming court. She doesn't have the time to worry about me.

By now, I've finished my drink, so I return to the kitchen to refill my punch glass. I just have it filled when I turn around and smack into something hard. The punch splashes in the cup, which sends red juice all over the front of my white dress. I look down at it in horror. The good news is that the Wright's white floor didn't take any of the damage, but that means I'm soaked.

"I am so sorry," the figure says.

I look up to see who I bumped into, and I find myself staring into Carter Hayes's blue eyes.

6

Here it is, my chance to finally talk to Carter. I open my mouth, but nothing comes out.

I want to curl up into a ball and die right about now. As if spilling punch all over myself isn't bad enough, it has to be in front of *him*. Carter grabs a pile of napkins from the counter and pats them on the punch stains.

Oh. My. God. I think he just touched my boob.

"I'm really sorry," he says again.

"No, I'm sorry," I manage to respond, but I can barely spit it out due to shock.

"Uh, this isn't going to work," Carter tosses the napkins in the trash. "Do you know where the bathroom is?"

I can't bring myself to say anything, so I shake my head instead, realizing a moment later that I just lied to him. I *do* know where the bathroom is, because this isn't my first time inside the Wright's house. I can't manage to correct myself.

"Here, I'll show you." Carter grabs my hand and leads me to the bathroom. My heart skips a beat, and all I can do is follow him.

We pass a photo in the hallway, and I pause to look at it. It's a picture of Ariel at six years old, hugging her dog Toby. The blonde of the golden retriever's coat matches Ariel's hair perfectly. I remember him. When we were friends, we'd play with him together all the time. I look at the caption of the photo, which lists Toby's birth and death dates. The death date is familiar. It's significant to me, but for other reasons.

"Hey." Carter's voice cuts through my thoughts. "This way."

I follow him as he tugs on my hand again. Carter hurries around the bathroom looking for something that will clean up the punch stains on my dress. I'm still in too much shock to say anything. I can't believe I'm alone in this room with Carter Hayes. Granted, the door is open, but still... there's no one else around. My heart speeds up thanks to my overactive nerves.

He wets a towel, and as he bends over the sink, I notice the pale blue light on the back of his neck. I lightly touch my own implant.

He hands me the wet towel. "Try this."

I wipe it across my dress, trying to get the stain out, but it doesn't work. I don't want to speak, but I hear words escape my mouth anyway, mostly out of curiosity.

"So, uh, your upgrade," I say. I don't meet his eyes, but a lump forms in my throat. I unwillingly give a cough to clear it. "How is it working for you?"

His hand moves onto the back of his neck. "It works great. I love the way music plays in your head. It took me a little off guard at first."

I nod. I can't believe he's talking to me like I'm a real person. "Me, too. So, nothing weird happened with yours?"

"No. Why? Did something weird happen with yours?"

"No," I say almost too quickly. My hands shake as I continue scrubbing away at my dress, my eyes locked on the big red stain. The stain isn't coming out, though. "It's just something my father would want to know about is all."

"Why do you hide it?" Carter asks.

His question surprises me. "Hide what?" I wonder.

"Your implant," he clarifies. "Don't get me wrong, your hair looks good down like that, but sometimes it seems like you're self-conscious about it."

Oh. Wow. Heat rises to my cheeks. I didn't know he

paid enough attention to notice. I can't *believe* that he would.

But I can't just tell him that I *am* insecure about. If it weren't for making my dad happy—and having the compatible appliances in my house—I would upgrade when everyone else does. But upgrading before everyone else makes me an oddity.

Except... Not this time. Not with Carter.

I stop wiping at my dress. "How come everyone cheered?" I find myself saying. I don't know where that came from, but I feel the need to explain my question. I let my eyes wander up to his face as I speak nervously. "In the lunchroom after you got your upgrade, everyone seemed to like the fact that you got a new implant. They weren't jealous or anything."

He shrugs. "I think a few of them were, but having the upgrade is cool, I guess. You know, people think your upgrades are always cool, too. People would ask you about it, but everyone is afraid to."

I snort. I actually, legitimately snort. My cheeks flame in embarrassment, and my hands shake against my dress as I go back to working the fruit punch out of it, attempting to avoid his gaze. "No, they wouldn't. They aren't scared of me. Everyone hates me. They hate me *because* of my upgrades."

"You really think that?" Carter asks. He looks me up

and down, then shakes his head. "That stain isn't going to come out. Here, take it off."

"What?" I can't believe what he just said. Carter Hayes just asked me to take off my clothes. I mean, it wasn't like *that*, but it still makes the nerves in my body ignite.

I look down at my dress and realize he's right. It's probably better to walk around in my bikini than a ruined dress. I slip it off, which makes me feel really awkward because his eyes are on me. I think I see them linger for a second.

He holds out his hand, and I give him my dress, even though I have no idea what he intends to do with it. He gestures for me to follow him, so I do. We walk down a long hallway and into a laundry room. It's a lot smaller than my laundry room, barely big enough for two people, so when we step inside, it feels cramped.

Carter smiles as he holds up a bottle of bleach. "This should do it," he says as he throws my dress and some bleach into the wash.

"You sure know your way around the Wright's house," I say, almost too softly because I still can't believe I'm alone with him.

He shrugs like it's nothing. "I used to date Ariel, so I'd come over a lot."

"Used to?" I ask, surprised at how bold I am at the

moment. Judging by the way Ariel still hangs on him, I assumed they were still together.

He nods as he shifts toward me slightly, and then his body presses up against mine. I freeze. What is going on? Is he *flirting* with me? Then I realize that he's only putting the bleach back on the shelf. We wouldn't be pressed up this close if the room wasn't so small. Still, I can't help but take in his scent and go weak in the knees.

"Oh. My. God."

Carter and I both look toward the hall where the voice came from. Trish Spencer, Ariel's right-hand lady, stands in the doorway. Of course, she had to choose the most inopportune moment to walk in on us.

Trish flees, and Carter chases after her. I follow quickly behind him.

When I reach the end of the hall, Carter is saying, "Come on, Trish. It wasn't like that."

Ariel stands in the kitchen with her arms crossed. Her lips are pressed into a thin line, and she glares at Carter.

"I was just helping her clean up from spilling juice all over her," Carter explains.

"You've *got* to be kidding me," Ariel says.

"They were totally making out," Trish accuses.

"We were not!" I defend, although what I really want to do is disappear. I can't believe this is happening to me.

I look around the room quickly, and everyone has stopped to watch the scene. It's not just people in the kitchen; everyone in the living room is looking on now, too.

"What are you even doing here, *Mila Brooks*?" Ariel snarls at me. She pronounces my name as if it's poison in her mouth.

I freeze. There are so many eyes on me right now. "I —uh." My quick breathing makes it hard to spit out my words. I choke on them. "Your announcement said anyone was invited." The lump rising in my throat causes my explanation to come out as a mere whisper.

"You didn't actually think that meant *you*, did you?" Ariel demands.

I open my mouth to speak, but I don't know what to say.

"News flash," Ariel says, "it didn't. I don't invite *losers* to my parties."

I'm keenly aware of all the other eyes on me, but I'm not sure if Ariel is. If she was, would she be saying such hurtful things and risk her chance at homecoming court? Or is this the kind of thing people like about her? I can't imagine why they would.

"Okay," I say meekly. My voice cracks, and I hate myself for letting that happen. It only shows my weakness. I don't dare open my mouth again.

I turn to leave, but Ariel doesn't seem like she's

finished yet. "If your loser boyfriend P.J. is here, you better take him with you."

I ball my hands into fists and want to turn back and smack her in the face, but I don't have the courage. I can't even turn back to correct her on J.P.'s name. Instead, I push through the crowd and rush outside toward my bike.

"Mila," a voice calls behind me. "Mila!" It's catching up.

I grip on to my bike's handlebars and swing the kickstand up with my foot. Firm hands grasp my shoulders. I try to push them away with a single hand, but he's strong, and I give up. I turn to see who chased me, and I find Carter standing over me once again.

"Come to make fun of me, too?" I ask with vengeance in my voice.

"What? No," he says, his eyes shifting between each of mine. "I just wanted to make sure you're okay. What Ariel said was really insensitive. If she didn't want everyone to come, she shouldn't have invited everyone. I just want you to know that we're not all like that."

I tear away from him and push my bike forward, swinging my leg over the seat.

"Come on, Mila," Carter says. "You can't ride home in just your swimming suit. I'll give you a ride."

"I don't want a ride," I tell him. I start pedaling to put distance between us.

From behind me, I hear him call out again, only I can't be sure of his words. "She only hates you because you're prettier than her."

I laugh internally. If only that were true. Ariel is the prettiest girl in school. Everyone loves her.

If it wasn't clear before, it's pretty clear now—I'm never going to fit in here.

7

By the time I arrive home, the humiliation still hasn't faded. Okay, so I was at her party, but is that any reason for Ariel to act so hostile toward me? What does she have against me, anyway?

I opt for a hot bubble bath to help me forget about the party. I turn on some peaceful music and let it play softly in my head.

A voice cuts through the music. "*Are you okay?*"

It's the same voice as before, and I'm not entirely sure what to make of it.

I somehow manage to answer, "No." And then I realize I'm talking to a stranger in my head. "And get out of my head!"

"*I only want to help,*" Parker says.

I figure I have a few options. If Parker is a real person and somehow managed to tap into my program, then I should be able to find some way to block him out. But what if he's just a figment of my imagination? What if I created him to deal with things like this? Or maybe he's *part* of the program. That makes sense. What if Parker is some sort of computer-generated emotional therapist or something?

"I, uh, just had a bad day," I try, wondering how much therapy I can get from the program—if that is, in fact, how it works. "I went to this party, and this girl humiliated me."

"*I told you not to go*," Parker says.

For a moment, I think about J.P. since he's the only one who told me not to go, but then I remember Parker said something about me not going, either. I think that's because deep down I knew something bad was going to happen if I ran into Ariel. And how could I not run into her in her own house? The program must have picked up on my worry and was trying to save me the trouble.

Suddenly, I find myself telling Parker all about the incident. I don't know where this newfound confidence comes from, but I think part of it is because I'm pretty sure he's not an actual person and that he's just part of the program. No way would I open up to someone like this in real life.

"I'm pretty sure I didn't hear him right," I continue, explaining to Parker about what I thought I heard Carter say as I rode away on my bike. "I mean, a guy like that wouldn't call me pretty."

"*Why not?*" Parker says in my head. "*It's the truth.*"

I scoff. "You're programed to say that to make me feel better."

"*Well, did it work?*"

I run my hand through the fading bubbles in my bath water and let a small smile form across my face. "Maybe a little," I admit.

"*Then I've done my job.*"

"Thank you for listening," I say with sincerity.

"*No problem. You can talk to me about anything.*"

I know our conversation is over, but I still think about Parker as I get out of the bath and dry myself off. If he really is a computer program, which makes the most sense, then I really can talk to him about anything. But even if talking makes me feel better, it's not like he's *real*. Even so, he seems to be the first person—*thing?*—in a long time that I can actually talk to.

A wave of nausea hits me as I dry my hair, and I grip on to the edge of the sink for support. I can feel a headache coming on, probably from stress. I get dressed and pop a few painkillers before crawling into bed much too early. I lay in bed for a while, replaying the events from earlier that day.

And then something hits me.

Before I went to the party, Parker said something

about leaving my hair down. And then at the party, Carter said he liked my hair down. What else did Carter say? He said I was beautiful. So did Parker. And their voices... They are similar.

Is it possible that Parker and Carter are the same person? Carter does have the upgrade. What if there is some psychic connection between us and our upgrades? What if they're connected somehow so that we can communicate in a different way than normal?

I sit up straight in my bed. I want to call out to Parker and learn more about him, but I lose my nerve when I consider that he might actually be Carter. The more I think about it, the more it makes sense. Except, why would Carter Hayes want to be inside my head and make me feel better?

I just want you to know that we're not all like that. That's what Carter said. Is it possible that he's trying to prove something? Maybe he feels like helping me will make him feel less like Ariel.

But that can't be right. Why me?

Besides, I don't *need* his help. It's not like I'm broken or anything.

Whoever Parker is, I wish he would stay out of my head.

8

Parker doesn't contact me at all on Sunday. I think about him a lot, but I'm able to take my mind off him with a long bike ride.

Later that night, my dad asks me about my implant. I don't tell him much because I'm not sure what Parker is yet, and I don't want to scare my father into thinking it's a glitch in the program. I try to coax out of him whether or not there's a therapist function, but I'm apparently too subtle because I don't get a clear answer.

At lunch on Monday, people stare at me again. I purposely leave my hair down to hide my implant, but something about the atmosphere in the room makes me want to curl up in a ball and disappear. I'm sure everyone is talking about how Ariel humiliated me on Saturday, but I'm lucky enough to sit at a corner table where I can turn away from all the watching eyes. It doesn't make the stares go away, but at least I can't see them.

I almost think that I'm overreacting and just being paranoid. Why would people care about me? But the nervous look on J.P.'s face tells me I have a reason to be suspicious of my peers.

"They're staring again, aren't they?" I ask J.P.

He nods and rubs his neck the way he always does. I give an involuntary shudder.

"It's not all bad," J.P. says. "They're probably considering voting you for homecoming court."

I gape at him. "What are you talking about?"

"After the way Ariel treated you on Saturday, who wants to vote for her?"

"So you heard about that?" I poke at my food and don't meet his gaze.

"Well, practically the whole school was there."

"Except for you," I point out.

"I was working," he defends.

I stare back down at my food and go silent again.

"By the way," J.P. adds. "I've been keeping an eye on your data like you asked. It looks like you've been stressed lately."

"Yeah," I agree. "With Ariel's party, I have been."

"Are you sure it's just stress?" His soft eyes almost don't meet mine, but when they do, he offers a light, encouraging smile.

I nod. "I've just been really stressed and embarrassed, I guess." That's enough to make him drop the subject.

As I leave the lunchroom, I catch Carter's eyes again. My heart flutters in my chest. Could he actually be Parker? I honestly don't know. A part of me almost wishes he is.

When I get home from school, I take another few painkillers and lock myself in my room to try contacting Parker. I just *have* to know who he is. Is he a real person? A figment of my imagination? A computer program? Carter...?

I cuddle up on my big cozy chair in the corner of my room and wrap a blanket around my body. I don't know how to make him appear in my head, so I call out a few times. "Parker, are you there?"

There isn't a response for a couple of minutes. I don't know what that means, but finally his voice rings clear in my head.

"*I'm here. Are you okay?*"

"I need to know who you are," I say.

"*I'm just a friend,*" he says, which only annoys me. I need the truth.

"But what are you? Are you a computer program, or are you a real person?"

"*I'm just here to listen.*"

My tolerance level is so short at the moment that I

want to explode. Why can't he give me a straight answer? That's not all that annoys me, though. All this stress has been building up in the last few days, giving me a pounding headache that I can't seem to shake. I'm exhausted, and all I want is for this headache to go away and to maybe actually spend time with someone my own age instead of secluding myself or hanging out with my mom.

"Fine," I say. "You say you're here to listen. Well, sit back and relax because it's going to take a while."

I don't consider who Parker really is as I divulge all my insecurities and secrets because it's easier that way. I let myself believe he isn't real, but another part of me nervously wants him to be Carter. There's something about his anonymity that makes the whole thing easier, though.

He stays so quiet that I'm not sure he's still there. A tear runs down my cheek as I tell him about all my problems gaining friends throughout the years and how alone that makes me feel. I don't let my voice waver, though, so I hope he doesn't notice.

"When I was in first grade, I had tons of friends," I tell him. "Even Ariel Wright was my friend, but then I got my first implant. I was the first one in my whole grade and the grade above me. At first, I thought my classmates would think it was cool, so I showed it off. Only, it made them jealous. For a few days, I was the talk of my class. Everyone wanted to see how my implant worked."

I sighed heavily. "And then Ariel stopped talking to me. She made up this stupid club, but I wasn't allowed because I had the implant. She promised cookies to all the members and even had this huge sleepover I wasn't invited to. I know it's really dumb because it was ten years ago, but thinking back on that, it still hurts."

I take a deep breath. "Are you still there?"

"*I'm still here*," Parker answers.

"The thing is that I've tried to make friends over the years. Just last Saturday I sat by a group of girls at Ariel's party. I don't think they wanted me there, though. They just talked about boys who I didn't know and didn't really acknowledge me."

"*What about J.P?*" Parker asks.

"J.P. is great and all, but we never have much to say to each other."

"*Maybe if you talked to him about things like this, he could be your friend.*"

I laugh because the idea sounds so ridiculous. "The only reason I'm opening up to you is because I don't know if you're human or not. Right now, it's easier to believe that you're just a computer program." I pause for a moment. "What are you?"

Just then, my watch buzzes. It's a message from my mom telling me it's dinner time.

My head still pounds as I rise from my chair. Only when I reach the dining room do I realize something. I never once mentioned J.P. to Parker.

That thought scares me, but it could honestly mean anything. It could mean Parker is someone I know, like Carter. Or it could mean the computer program can read my thoughts outside of what I share with it. Or it could just mean Parker is a part of my subconscious and he already knew about J.P.

I try a more direct approach with getting answers from my father at dinner. "Dad?"

"Yeah?" he asks with a full mouth.

"Can I ask you a hypothetical question?"

"Sure," he says with narrowed eyes, like he doesn't know where I'm going with this.

"Let's say that you created an upgrade that had a therapist application."

He stops with his fork halfway to his mouth. "That's actually a really good idea. I'm going to bring that one up with the team."

Okay. Well, that at least tells me Parker isn't part of a computer therapist program. Dad would know about him otherwise.

"Well, I was thinking, if you had something like that, would the program be able to read your thoughts?"

Dad cocked an eyebrow. "You're not turning into a conspiracy theorist, are you?"

"What? No. I'm just saying..."

"I suppose in theory, a program like that could. I mean, we're able to transfer simple thoughts into commands, so why not be able to read your thoughts? But the ethics committee would never allow that. We would especially never allow a program like that to store your thoughts that you didn't share with it freely."

I nod in understanding, but I still have so many questions. I want to tell my dad about Parker, but what if he isn't a result of the implant? What if he's just a figment of my imagination? I have to know for myself first before I go screwing up my dad's data.

"I've also been wondering about the call function on our implants. Would it ever be possible to create a sort of psychic link between two people so they could communicate on a different level than what we have now?" I wonder.

"What do you mean?" he asks.

I think about how when Parker talks to me in my head, it feels different than when Mom and I tested out our calling function. "Could they communicate directly through the program, more efficiently? Maybe by thinking things to each other rather than by speaking out loud."

"I suppose in theory, it would work, but we aren't that far yet. Why the sudden interest?"

"I, uh, have just been thinking about my implant and want to understand the extent of its capabilities."

That seems like enough of an explanation for my father, and he goes back to eating.

I'm not entirely sure what these answers mean in regards to Parker. He can't be a computer program since he knew about J.P. when I never said anything, right? Or, what if an error slipped through the ethics committee? But Dad said they didn't have that type of therapist program. He also said they were far away from creating types of psychic connections. I have no idea what to make of this. That means he's just a figment of my imagination, right? But he feels so genuine.

I go to bed thinking about Parker and the possibilities of his identity. If I don't learn his identity soon, I'll have to mention this to my dad. My implant will be removed while the company looks into it...

I find myself thinking that maybe that isn't such a bad thing.

9

I wake on Tuesday feeling like I know less about Parker's identity than I did the night before. This only frustrates me and makes the ache in my head pulse more intensely. I want to know. I *have* to know.

Maybe I already do...

Carter, I decide. It has to be him.

I mean, it makes the most sense. Mahone hasn't even come up with the idea for a computer-generated therapist, so that can't be it. Carter has the implant like me, and it's still in the testing stage. There must be a glitch that connects us.

Then there's always the possibility that I'm crazy and making Parker up, but that doesn't explain why some things Parker said matched up with some things Carter said, like calling me pretty.

I let out a soft laugh at that thought as I get ready for school. If Carter thinks I'm pretty, he has to be the only one. It's just not possible that two guys would say the same thing to me in the same day.

But I still have to know for sure. I could confront Carter at school. Or maybe it's best to talk with Parker about his identity while I'm in private.

Later that day, I sit silently at my lunch table and still haven't worked up the courage to confirm my suspicions. I avoid all gazes and poke at my food. Across the table, I can see J.P. in my peripheral vision doing that thing he does where he opens his mouth like he's going to speak and then closes it again.

I start to get annoyed. He must have opened his mouth six times already without saying anything. Normally I don't mind, but my headache makes every little thing seem more annoying.

"What?" I snap more aggressive than I mean to.

J.P. looks taken aback and blinks a few times. He rests his hand on the side of his neck as he speaks. "I—I'm just worried about you. You don't look good."

Of course I don't. My head is pounding, and I'm pretty sure I've started sweating. I've been really stressed out lately.

"I'm fine," I tell him.

"Are you sure? Because you look pretty pale."

"Yes, J.P. I'm fine. It's just a headache." I grit my teeth. It's nice he cares, but I don't understand why he does.

When he doesn't say anything else, I stand to dump my tray. My headache is only getting worse, and I feel like I need a moment outside the noisy lunchroom. I recycle my tray and am headed for the cafeteria exit past Ariel's table when my feet catch on something, and I'm sent flying. I stick my hands out to catch myself, and they make a loud smack on the hard floor as I tumble down.

Laughter erupts from around me. I look toward my feet to see what I tripped on. One of the guys at Ariel's table grins down at me mischievously, and it's obvious he did it on purpose. People stand to get a good look at me on the ground, and their eyes all glare at me judgmentally. I feel like disappearing. Just as I'm about to push myself up and run off, a figure approaches and stands above me. I lift my head slowly, and Ariel stares back at me, her hands on her hips.

"Is your implant throwing off your balance?" Ariel asks in the fakest voice I've ever heard.

Great, I think. *Go right after my implant, why don't you?*

All I want to do is run from the lunchroom. Everybody's eyes are on Ariel and me. I'm not sure if I should get out of here as soon as possible like I feel like doing or actually stand up to her. I decide to flee, because it will only be easier.

As I pull myself up and get ready to run, Ariel starts talking again. "Don't forget to tell your daddy about this. I'm sure he can build in a coordination function just for you for your next upgrade."

People snicker from the table next to me.

I do my best to let it go, but the headache pounding on the sides of my skull makes me bold. Ariel just pulled the last straw.

"I'll be sure to tell him about it," I say, and I pause just long enough that a smirk forms across Ariel's face. "Then he can build in an anti-bitch function for you."

Everyone in the lunchroom inhales a simultaneous breath. A few people let out noises that confirm I just crossed some sort of line, but I hardly notice. I can't believe I said that. Ariel opens her mouth to say something back, but I'm already turning away.

I push through the cafeteria doors and head toward the bathrooms. Right now, the stress headache that has been plaguing me for days is too intense to make anything else matter. I want to revel in my little bout of courage and success, but I lean up against a wall instead and take a deep breath.

"Mila." I hear a voice behind me.

For a second, I think it's Parker, but when I turn, I find it was Carter who spoke my name.

It has to be him, I think. *It only makes sense.*

"Parker," I say in a near whisper. What I really mean to do is ask him if he is Parker, but confronting Ariel made me lose all my nerve.

"Look," Carter says, "it was wrong of Ariel to pick on you like that. To be honest, it was really cool what you did back there. She needs someone to tell her off every once in a while."

I narrow my eyes a bit. I can't figure him out. So what if he is Parker? What would he want with me?

"Why are you doing this? Why do you care about me?" I raise my eyes sheepishly to meet his gaze.

Carter looks confused for a second, like he's not sure why I don't get it. "I want you to know that you don't deserve the way Ariel treats you. I'll admit it. I didn't care much until I got the upgrade this time around. I guess since we both have it, I feel a sort of connection with you, you know?"

I do, I think. He has to be talking about how our implants are linked, only his words bring up another question. If he knew about the connection, why did he give me a different name? Why didn't he just tell me he was Carter to begin with and we could have sorted out the connection earlier? Unless I heard him wrong...

"I don't think it's fair that people treat you the way they do," Carter adds. "As a fellow beta tester, I feel this need to let them see that, and maybe let you see that there are people in this school who want to hang out with you."

"Why didn't you just tell me your real name to begin with?" I blurt. Seriously, I still can't figure him out.

He looks momentarily confused, but the next moment, I don't have the energy to focus on his answer.

"I'm going to be sick," I announce, and I immediately race for the bathroom. Since it's a ladies' room only, Carter doesn't follow. I hear him ask if I'm okay through the door, and I assure him I'll be fine on my own.

I stay hunched over the toilet for a few minutes until the bell rings. Although I'm starving now, I'm relieved that my little episode helped clear my head for the most part.

But that doesn't seem to be the end of my troubles. As the day goes on, it seems more and more people are talking about my confrontation with Ariel. Nobody says anything directly to me, but I can tell that people are whispering about it in my afternoon classes.

Later that afternoon, Parker's—*Carter's?*—voice resonates through my head. "*Are you okay, Mila?*"

I look around nervously. I can't talk with him here, not in front of all these people. *Not now*, I want to say to Parker.

"Now's as good of time as ever," he says, and I'm completely taken off guard.

You can hear my thoughts? I ask without speaking out loud. I look around again, but I don't think anyone else can tell what's going on.

"Only what you want me to hear," he tells me.

Right now, I want you out of my head, I think at him. My headache is starting to come back, and I really don't think the middle of a mathematics lecture is the right time to be having this conversation.

"I'm just trying to help," he says.

I breathe an audible sigh. *I understand,* I say truthfully. *But I don't know how much I want to talk about what happened earlier today.*

"I'm sorry. You're in class. I shouldn't have bothered you right now. Will you tell me about it later?"

I crack a light smile at how sincere and kind he sounds. He really does sound concerned for me, but how can I talk to him now when I'm supposed to be taking notes? Math isn't exactly my best subject—history is my favorite—so I try to pay extra attention in this class.

Yes, I tell him. *We can talk about it later.*

A small part of me expects Carter to meet up with me sometime after school to finish talking to me, but I don't spot him the rest of the day. I'm partially relieved that I don't have to talk with him, but another part of me wants to get to the bottom of our *connection.*

By the end of the day, Carter's nowhere in sight, so I hop on my bike and pedal home.

If nothing else, I can finally escape my classmates' stares, but it doesn't give me the comfort that I hope for.

10

When I arrive home, I don't even say hello to my mom before I fall into bed and curl into a ball. That's something I've wanted to do all day Not only was tripping in the lunchroom and having everyone laugh at me humiliating enough, but then I had to go tell Ariel off. That only seemed to add fuel to the fire and make things worse.

I won't go to school tomorrow. I can't, right? I pull the bed sheet above my head and want nothing more than to fall asleep and forget my troubles. but just then, Parker's voice cuts through the silence.

"Are you ready to talk about what happened?"

I sigh. I suppose I should talk about it. or I'll just end up with a worse headache than I already have.

"You were there," I say out loud. "You saw how bad it was."

"It wasn't as bad as you think it was, Mila. You came off looking like the good guy."

"I don't know about that. I felt humiliated."

"You're not the first person Ariel has humiliated."

I guess he had a point. "But how does everyone else get past it?" I ask. "They're all different than me. Everyone else actually has friends to talk to about this kind of stuff."

"So do you."

I scoff. "In case you haven't been paying attention, I don't have any friends."

"You have me," he says in a way that nearly melts my heart.

"You think we're friends?"

"Of course we are," he says.

I can't believe what I'm hearing. Carter thinks we're friends? He really meant what he said about feeling connected to me, didn't he?

"If we're friends," I say, "then you'll help me take my mind off all this, right?"

"Anything to make you feel better," he answers. *"By the way, how are you feeling?"*

"Just a headache," I say, but I immediately jump into something more exciting. "I always feel better after reading about or watching documentaries on history. My dad's really big into old technology—says it shows him where he's going with Mahone—and so I kind of get into it in a big way like he does."

"*I know*," Carter says. I notice for a moment how I've started thinking of him as Carter instead of Parker.

I excitedly hop out of bed and head toward my bookshelf that's filled with historical books and articles I printed off. I tell him all these wonderful stories about how people used to live their lives and what they used to eat.

"French fries," I say. As I dive further into our conversation, I realize how comfortable I'm getting with him. That hardly seems possible. *Me?* Not only talking with Carter but feeling like I *can?*

"They were these deep-fried potato wedges people would eat all the time with their hamburgers," I continue, "and because they were so high in calories, they made people gain weight. But I've read about healthy foods, too. There were peanut butter and jelly sandwiches. They're kind of like those sweet sandwiches we sometimes have at lunch, but people would spread the peanut butter and jelly on their bread themselves. I don't know what it tastes like, but I bet it's good. I wonder where you can get peanut butter nowadays. Do you think they still make it somewhere?"

The question is rhetorical, but Carter answers anyway. "*I bet they do. You realize people still make food from scratch, right?*"

"What?" I ask flatly. If they did, why hasn't my mom —who enjoys as much cooking as she can get—figured out how to make things from scratch?

"*Well, where do you think your food comes from?*" He had me there.

I think about it for a second. "I guess people do have to farm the food like they did in the old days. I haven't really thought about how much work would go into it."

"*Maybe we could take an adventure someday and see the farm fields for ourselves,*" Carter suggests.

I nearly choke. Is he asking me on a date? Or is he suggesting we take some sort of vacation down the road? I find that somewhat unbelievable. "You can't be serious."

"*Why not?*"

"Guys like you don't ask for things like that from girls like me. What are you playing at?"

"*What do you mean, guys like me?*"

"We don't mix, Carter. I know you said that thing about our implants, but—"

"*You think I'm Carter? Carter Hayes?*"

I freeze for a moment. The realization that I got it wrong sends the pounding in my head into overdrive. "You mean, you're not?"

"*Not Carter Hayes? I told you my name is Parker.*"

I think back to school and rack my brain trying to pinpoint exactly who Parker could be. I don't think I know any Parker, yet he acted like he saw what happened in the lunchroom, and he knows who Carter Hayes is, so he has to be someone from school, right? But I don't know everyone's names. Is there even a Parker at my school?

Parker... Parker who?

"You're not the guy who sits at the lunch table next to mine and picks his nose, are you?" I ask, almost horrified.

"*Nope, not him.*"

I can't think of any Parker. "Then what are you? A part of my subconscious? A computer program?"

"*I think it's best if I told you in person,*" he says.

So that confirms it. He is a real person. But *who?* And how?

"Are you the kid in my math class who's a grade younger than me? I hear he's good at hacking into computers."

"*Mila, if you haven't figured it out by now, you never will. Meet me at the Fountain at six, and I'll explain everything.*"

"Okay," I agree.

My head pounds hard in anticipation, but I manage to crawl out of bed and make my way to my car in the garage a few hours later. I tell it to drive me to the Fountain. I have to figure out who Parker is.

I park my car along the street and make my way over

to the water fountain in the center of the courtyard. I look around and wonder which guy could be Parker, but no one catches my eye. Maybe he's not here yet.

Then I see him.

J.P. walks toward me, and I have the thought that it can't be him. It wasn't his voice in my head. He would've had to manipulate the program—

My thoughts stop dead in their tracks when I realize he's able to do just that. J.P. works at Mahone and has access to my data. Dad said Mahone can't store data on people's thoughts, but what if J.P. can see it in real-time?

Anger flares through my body. *"You're* Parker?" I demand as he approaches.

"Please, let me explain," J.P. begs. He reaches out for me, but I take a step away from him.

"What's there to explain?" I sneer. "You hacked into my implant! How *dare* you!?"

I shove him hard, but he's so much bigger than me that he barely moves.

"I didn't hack your implant," J.P. says. "You asked me to take a look at your data. I never would've accessed it if you didn't ask. When I went in, I found a vulnerability in the program that allowed me to talk to you. I said I'd help you, and I thought trying to talk to you was the best way."

I can hardly believe what I'm hearing. Betrayal cuts through me like a knife. "You should've reported the vulnerability to Mahone, and instead you took advantage of it!"

"I'm sorry," J.P. insists. "I really am. I just wanted you to know you're not alone, but you'd never talk to me face-to-face. I thought I could help by being your friend, but it's clear now you never wanted that. I messed up. If you never want to see me again, I understand. Just know... I wanted to be friends."

I take another step back, and my leg touches the edge of the fountain. "After what you did, we will *never* be friends."

The pounding in my head seems almost audible now and feels as if something is trying to escape. *Pound, pound, pound* on the side of my skull. The bustle of the city and the voices in the courtyard fade to near nonexistence as the pain takes over. I feel like I'm panting for air, but I can't be sure.

My head swirls, and I start to get hot like I'm going to hurl. Then, the world starts moving unnaturally. In what feels like slow motion, the fountain closes in on me. I'm briefly aware of the water as it envelops me, of the chill on my skin and the sting as I inhale and water rushes into my lungs, but there's nothing I can do about it. I don't even realize what's happening.

I feel strong hands grip my wrists, but that's it before everything goes black.

11

I'm aware that time has passed, but I don't know how much. I blink a few times until the bright lights above my head come into focus. I'm lying on my back on a bed, and my headache is completely gone. I look to my right to assess my surroundings and spot my watch on the table next to me. I mentally tell it to bring up my GPS location so I can figure out where I am, but nothing happens.

I prop myself up on my elbows to get a better look at the room. It's small with stark white walls, and there's a door with a big window that lets me see out into a hallway. I must be in some sort of hospital room. I can remember passing out, but I don't recall how I got here.

Outside the door, J.P. stands with his back toward me, and he's talking to a nurse. His hand cups the side of his neck the way it always does. After a moment, he turns and locks his gaze on me. Deep regret crosses his features.

Good. He should feel bad.

J.P. opens the door and takes an apprehensive step into the room.

"Why do you do that thing?" I ask as he enters the room.

He looks momentarily confused.

"With your neck," I clarify. "You always rub your neck with your right hand."

Realization spreads across his face. 'It's just something I do when I'm nervous."

"But you *always* do it. Are you always nervous?"

He moves across the room and pulls one of the chairs closer to my bed. He sits in it and adjusts himself quietly before answering. "I'm always nervous around you."

"You shouldn't be. We've known each other for years."

"I know, but sometimes it's hard to talk to you," he admits.

"How so?" I ask, honestly curious.

J.P. hesitates, then finally says, "You shut people out, Mila."

I recoil. "I don't *shut people out*. People just don't want to talk to me. In case you haven't noticed, J.P., everyone hates me."

"No, they don't," he insists. "You just don't let anyone else in."

"Name one time," I challenge.

"Those girls at Ariel's pool party. They welcomed you and probably would have been your friends if you didn't run away."

I'm stunned that he found an example so quickly. "That doesn't count. Those girls didn't even want to talk to me."

"You can't be sure of that," he says. "What about me? Like you said, we've known each other for years, yet we still can't talk to each other."

I cross my arms and say bitterly, "You've ruined any chance of that after what you did. What are you still doing here?"

"I wanted to make sure you're all right," he replies. "Your parents are on the way. They should be here soon."

He looks like he wants to leave, but I'm curious about one more thing. I need to know.

"Why did you choose the name Parker?" I ask. "In my head, you told me your name was Parker, but it didn't sound like you at all."

"I told you my name was Parker because it is. My full name is Jason Parker Thompson. My dad's name is Jason, too, so at home, my mom calls me Parker. She never liked the J.P. nick name. My voice changed because of the way the computer program transmitted the data."

"You never should've tried to talk to me," I say.

I want to tell him to get out of the room. I want to pull the implant out of the back of my head. I want to—

Wait. The implant...

I reach up to feel the back of my neck, but it's completely smooth. Panic sweeps through my body. I start to push myself up from the bed. "What happened to my implant?"

"It's fine," J.P. assures me. "The doctors took it out."

I lean back until my head touches the pillow again. I haven't lived without my implant since I was six. Having nothing at the base of my skull is nerve-racking.

I look up at J.P. "Why would they do that?"

"You weren't well, Mila," he says. "I told the doctors about the abnormalities with your chip, and about your headaches. They had no idea it could cause issues like this, and they thought it best to remove the implant for now. It's a good thing, because they said it was making you sick. You'll get the most recent approved version— the one you had before—after you get out of here. They figure the new technology coupled with your stress caused the headaches, but the version you had before should be fine."

"Am I the first case?" I ask.

"It looks like you're the third reported one, but it

seems like there's only a connection with this current version and stress. We haven't even rolled out this version to all the beta testers. The project's getting put on hold."

"Good," I state. "It should be. No one should have access to someone else's mind like that."

"The data that's shared with Mahone is all within the user agreement," J.P. says. "We don't have access to everything. I can see things like your heart rate and what you're searching online in real-time as long as you're connected to your watch. That doesn't make it right, though. I never should've agreed to check your data in the first place. What I did was wrong, and I understand if you don't ever want to talk to me again. I'm going to report the vulnerabilities to Mahone, then I'm going to leave my apprenticeship."

That makes me really sad, because I don't want J.P. losing his job. What he did was wrong, but I worry he'd have never discovered the vulnerabilities in the program if he hadn't checked my data like I asked. Something had been wrong with my implant since the day I got it. I recall the heart rate spike I had when I woke up from surgery, and the chill that I felt in the shower later that day. Add in the headaches, and it's clear the implant has been screwing with my nervous system all this time. If J.P. hadn't found the vulnerability in my implant, the doctors wouldn't have removed it. He could've very well saved my life.

I don't know why I feel bad for him, after what he did. If anything, I should be happy he's getting what he deserves. But I know working at Mahone is everything he ever wanted, and I don't want to see my friend give up on his dreams.

I go completely still when I realize I just thought of him as my friend. It's strange, because for so long I never thought of us as friends. Is that what we'd become? I think of how easy it was to talk to him when he was in my head, and how natural it felt. Maybe I really did need a friend all this time.

As I look up at him, I realize that as much as I tell myself we aren't friends, I care very deeply for J.P., and it's obvious he cares for me, too. Perhaps I was too hard on him.

"Have you ever accessed anyone else's data?" I ask.

J.P. shakes his head. "No, and I wouldn't have done it if you didn't ask. I should've just stopped there, before I ever found the vulnerability. There's nothing I can say to justify it. I just hope that you start feeling better now that your implant's out. I'll let you rest now."

J.P. stands to leave the room, but I stop him.

"J.P., wait. You're right. I *do* need to open up to people. What you did... it isn't what friends do. But maybe we could try again, on new terms."

He furrows his brow. "What kind of terms?"

"Never—and I mean *never*—use Mahone's system to get in my head again," I state clearly.

He nods. "Never. I promise."

"And from now on... I'll open up to everyone. But you're not allowed to tell me who I get to speak to, or when I can and can't go to a party."

"Fair," he agrees. "I didn't want you to go because I didn't want Ariel hurting you, but I should've trusted that you can handle yourself."

"So... friends?" I ask.

He nods. "Friends."

I reach out a hand, and we shake on it.

"Oh," he says, pulling away. "I got you something." He turns toward the other end of the room and comes back with a plastic bag. There's something brown inside, but I can't tell what it is. He hands it to me, and all I can do is stare.

"Is this a—"

"Peanut butter and jelly sandwich?" His hand runs along his neck again, but then he abruptly stops when he realizes what he's doing. "Yeah, it is."

12

When I go back to school, all eyes are on me again. This time, I know exactly why. I wear my dark hair up in a high ponytail, and it shows off the nape of my neck perfectly. Today, I'm not different because I have a new implant. This time, it's because I don't have one at all.

I'll get it put back in someday, once Mahone patches the vulnerabilities in the program, but for now, things seem simpler and easier without it, and I'm not afraid to show that off proudly.

Carter catches up with me on my way to the cafeteria. "Mila," he calls.

I turn to meet his gaze. He hasn't met up with his group of friends yet, so he's all alone.

"How are you doing?" he asks. "Last time I saw you, you didn't look well."

"Much better," I assure him. "Thanks for checking."

He shoves his hands in his pockets. "That's what friends are for, right?"

I smile. "Friends?"

He shrugs, but there's hope in his expression. "If you want. I'm having a party at my house this weekend. You're welcome to come."

My heart warms at the invitation. "I'd love to."

"That's great to hear. I'll see you around." He starts to walk away, but then turns back like he's forgotten something. "Oh, and if Ariel asks like a jerk again, just let me know, and I'll talk to her."

"It's okay," I start to say.

"I really mean it," he interrupts.

"If something happens, I'll handle it myself," I promise.

I turn to the cafeteria with a smile on my face, but I should've known that showing my confidence would hit a chord with Ariel. As I'm getting into the lunch line, a pain tugs at my skull. I whirl around to face my attacker. My hair falls down around my shoulders, and Ariel tightly grips my elastic in her palm. I can't help but think of how childish she's being.

"I see your dad is working on that balance thing, then. Took the whole implant out to fix it," she sneers.

All I want to do is punch her in the face, but I take a

deep breath instead. I don't know if she's realized it, but the lunchroom has gone silent, and all eyes are on us.

"I know why you hate me," I say.

Ariel's face contorts into a confused expression. She was hoping I'd retaliate more hostilely, no doubt.

"*What?*" she spits.

"I know why you hate me," I repeat. 'It's because I wasn't there when Toby died, isn't it?"

Ariel scoffs. "He was just a dog, and that was ten years ago. You can't expect me to still be mad about that."

Trish looks around the room at everyone staring at us. She nervously pulls on Ariel's wrist. "Let's just go."

Ariel doesn't take her eyes off me, though.

"I saw the picture of him in your house," I admit. "You loved Toby. You thought I wasn't there because I was getting my implant, didn't you?"

I realize now that's why she always hated me for my implant.

Ariel looks around the room, like she can't believe we're having this conversation. "Okay, so I guess I was mad. We had a funeral and everything, and you weren't there."

"You never told me he died," I say.

"You had to know! I vividly remember my mom talking to your mom on the phone about it, and then you just never showed up. Your family thought it was better that you got that implant than to be with your best friend in a time of need."

I let out a breath in disbelief. "That wasn't it at all! I got the implant the day before. I remember because the date on that picture in your house was the same day my mom broke her tibia."

Ariel blinks a few times in shock. There's a long pause where nobody makes a noise. "I'm so sorry," she finally says. "I don't know how I didn't realize."

"You never let me explain. You just stopped talking to me."

We stand there in silence for a few seconds. It's so quiet in the lunchroom that I wouldn't be surprised if you could literally hear a pin drop.

"Truce?" I offer, sticking my hand out to her.

She eyes my hand nervously, like she's unsure. Then she smiles and shakes my hand. "Truce," she agrees. Whatever damage I did to her chance at homecoming representative, I think I've just redeemed her. The cool thing is that I'm perfectly happy with that.

Afterward, the chatter in the lunchroom returns. Ariel and I aren't exactly best friends, but at least we understand each other now.

I set my food across from J.P. like normal, but today I scan the lunchroom instead of shying away from it. I spot a group of girls a few tables away and notice some empty seats near them.

"Want to try a new spot today?" I ask J.P.

He follows my gaze and gives a wide smile in agreement. We pick up our trays and make our way over to the empty chairs. A girl with pale skin and short red hair laughs with her friends and doesn't notice our approach.

"Kaya?" I ask, tapping her on the shoulder.

She looks up expectantly but has the same welcoming smile on her face as she did the first time I asked the question.

"Do you mind if we sit here?" I ask.

She scoots over to make room. "No problem! We'd love to have more people at our table."

J.P. and I exchange a smile as we sit down side by side at our new table.

"Mila," he says lightly.

My heart flutters at the sound of my name. I think about how Carter used to make my heart swoon, but as I steal a glance over at his table, I only feel joy for the kindness he showed me. There's no room for lust in my heart.

I look back at J.P. and realize how much sense it makes the he was Parker all along. How could I think it would be anyone else?

"I just wanted you to know that I'm really proud of you," J.P. says.

"Thank you. I'm pretty proud of myself, too." I reach out and take J.P.'s hand. "Thanks for being here for me."

I squeeze his hand lightly and smile as I realize that this is only the beginning of our friendship.

THE END

ABOUT THE AUTHOR

Alicia Rades is a USA Today bestselling author of young adult and new adult paranormal fiction. This is her first sci-fi story. When she's not dreaming up magical stories, she's either binge-watching Netflix, meditating, or spending time with her family. She has an unhealthy obsession with psychic characters and writes with a deck of tarot cards next to her computer.